Bat and Sloth
Hang Around

To Dave and Ellen—
I love hanging around with you both!
LK

To Elijah
SB

Library of Congress Cataloging-in-Publication data
is on file with the publisher.

Text copyright © 2020 by Leslie Kimmelman
Illustrations copyright © 2020 by Albert Whitman & Company
Illustrations by Seb Braun
First published in the United States of America in 2020
by Albert Whitman & Company
ISBN 978-0-8075-0585-4 (hardcover)
ISBN 978-0-8075-0584-7 (ebook)

Printed in China
10 9 8 7 6 5 4 3 2 1 WKT 24 23 22 21 20 19

Design by Rick DeMonico

For more information about Albert Whitman & Company,
visit our website at www.albertwhitman.com.

Bat and Sloth
Hang Around

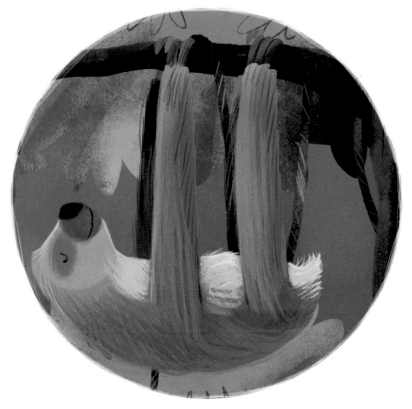

illustrated by
Leslie Kimmelman   **Seb Braun**

Albert Whitman & Company
Chicago, Illinois

Making Friends

The sky was light.
The air was warm, wet, and sweet.
Deep in a forest, a fruit bat hung
upside down.

It grew dark.

Time to wake up!

Bat's eyes popped open.

Eek!

Something was on the tree beside him.

"This is *my* branch!" he said to the

something.

The something yawned.
"Can't we share it?" he replied.
"What are you?" asked Bat.
"I am a two-toed sloth,"
said Sloth slowly.

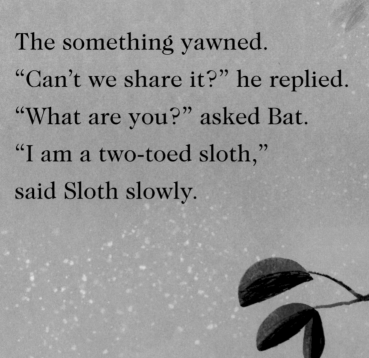

"Why should we share a branch?"
said Bat.
"We have nothing in common."
"Yes we do," protested Sloth.
"Like what?" asked Bat, flapping.
"I have long, beautiful wings.
You have no wings at all."

"True," said Sloth.
"I have fur. And strong claws,"
he added.

"I am fast," said Bat.

He zipped. He zapped.

"I am faster than a jet plane. You are not."

"True," said Sloth, yawning.

"I am SUPER slow."

Sloth stretched and smiled.
"But," he said, "we both like
hanging around."
"That's true," said Bat,
"and upside-down."
"From the same branch," said Sloth.
Bat looked at Sloth.
"From the same branch," he agreed.

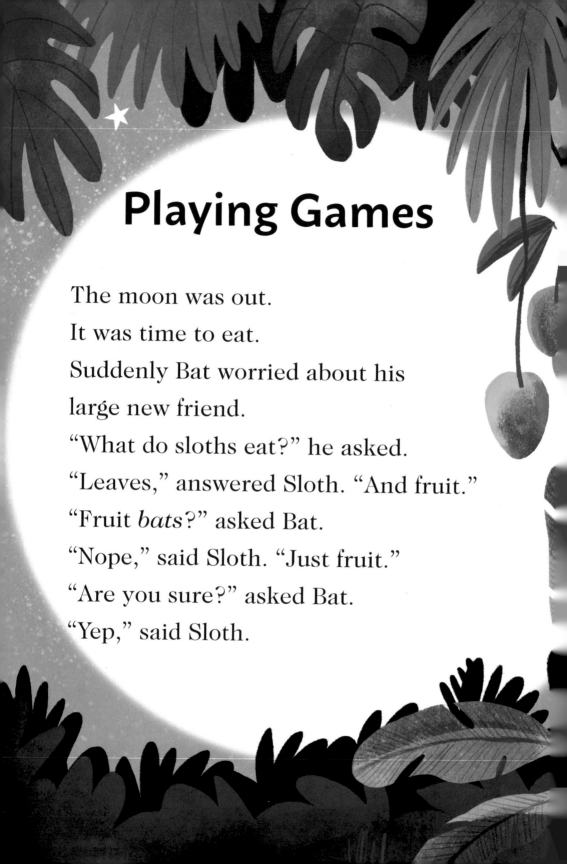

Playing Games

The moon was out.

It was time to eat.

Suddenly Bat worried about his large new friend.

"What do sloths eat?" he asked.

"Leaves," answered Sloth. "And fruit."

"Fruit *bats*?" asked Bat.

"Nope," said Sloth. "Just fruit."

"Are you sure?" asked Bat.

"Yep," said Sloth.

Bat and Sloth ate avocados.

"Yum," said Bat.

They bit bananas.

"Delicious," said Bat.

They munched mangoes.

"Sweet," said Bat.

"Are we friends?" asked Bat. "Because if we are friends, we should get to know each other."

"Okay," said Sloth.

"Well," began Bat, "We both like night, and trees, and fruit."

"Yep," Sloth agreed.

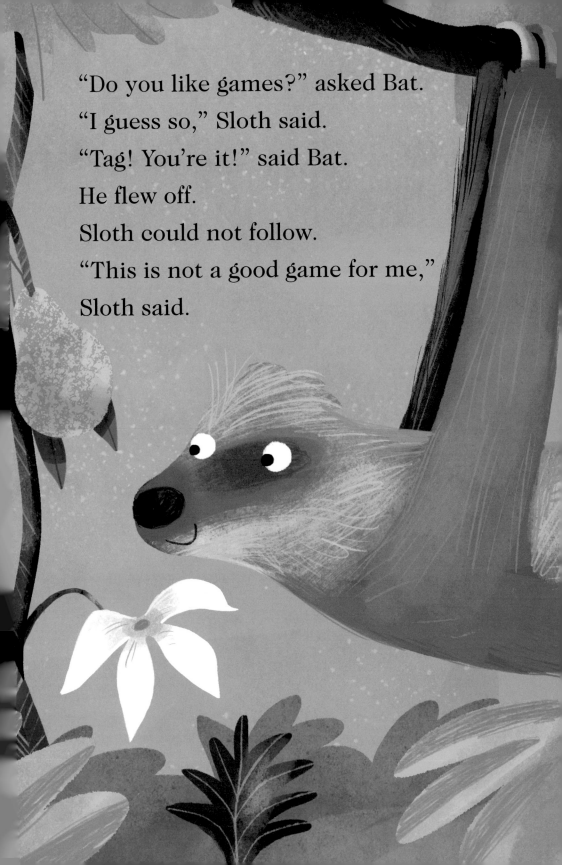

"Do you like games?" asked Bat.

"I guess so," Sloth said.

"Tag! You're it!" said Bat.

He flew off.

Sloth could not follow.

"This is not a good game for me,"
Sloth said.

"We can play hide-and-seek," said Bat.
"You count to ten. I will hide."
Sloth counted to ten
V-E-R-Y S-L-O-W-L-Y.
It was more like counting to a
hundred.

The stars went out.
Bat waited.
The sun began to rise.
Bat waited some more.

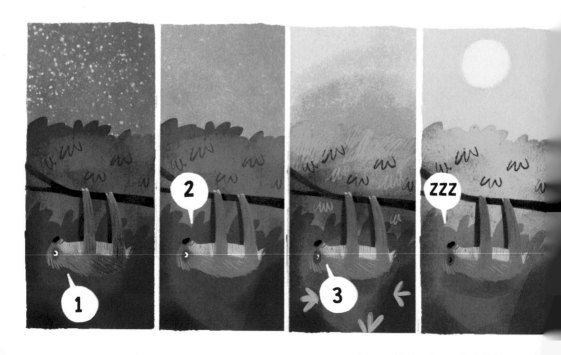

Finally Bat came out from his
hiding place.
Sloth was asleep on their branch.
Bat hung upside down beside his
new friend.
"We both like to sleep," mumbled
Bat sleepily.
ZZAahhchhhzzz, went Sloth.
"But only one of us snores," Bat added.

Being Heroes

One night Sloth was eating leaves.
Suddenly he froze.
A harpy eagle was circling in the sky.
"Oh no!" said Sloth. "Don't let that
eagle see us.
To him, I am not Sloth.
I am dinner."

Gurgle bubble gurgle bubble.
"Shh," hushed Bat. "Keep your
voice down."
"That is not my voice," said Sloth.
"That is my stomach. My stomach
sings when I eat!"
The bird circled lower.
"Who's there?" Eagle called.
"It's just me," answered Bat.
"I am stretching my wings.
Ahh, that feels good."

"Who's gurgling?" asked Eagle.

He was ready to SWOOP!

Bat felt Sloth shaking under his wings.

"That's my stretching song,"
Bat said quickly.

He sang. "Gurgle, bubble, gurgle,
bubble, s-t-r-e-t-c-h!"

"You are a very weird bat," said Eagle.

But he flew away.

Sloth crawled out.
"You are a hero, Bat.
And you are my friend for life."
Bat had never been called
a hero before.
He zipped and zapped happily.
He zipped and zapped high.
He zipped and zapped low.

Too low. Bat fell in the river.

"Help!" he cried. "Fruit bats can't swim!"

"Sloths can swim," said Sloth.

Sloth plopped down from the branch
into the river.

Splash!

"You are a hero, too," said Bat.
Later, he made up a song.
"Two heroes on a tree," he sang.
"One is you, and two is me."
Sloth said, "Don't make a fuss."
Then he added softly, "Hooray for us!"

Things that Go BUMP in the Night

Zip! Zap!

Bat was very fast.

Zip! Smack!

He bumped into Sloth,

who was hanging from their branch.

Ompff!

Sloth looked up at Bat.

"Don't you have something to say?"

asked Sloth.

"You *always* have something to say."

But Bat was silent.

"You bumped me off the branch!"
said Sloth.

"Did not!" said Bat.

"I was zipping and zapping.
I was *not* bumping."

"If it wasn't you, then who was it?"
asked Sloth.

"A spider monkey?" suggested Bat.

"Hmm," said Sloth.

"A nine-banded armadillo?"
suggested Bat.

"Hmm," said Sloth.

"A kinkajou?" suggested Bat.

"Hmm," said Sloth.

Bat sighed. "Okay, maybe it was me.
But you were in my way."
Sloth smiled all the time.
But he was not smiling now.
Bat sighed. "Sorry if I bumped you,"
he said.

"IF you bumped me?" said Sloth.

"You *did* bump me."

"Okay already," said Bat. "Sorry."

Sloth looked at him.

"You don't *sound* sorry,"
said Sloth finally.

His voice was sad.

Bat's zaps lost their zip.
"I *am* sorry," he told Sloth. "Really.
Do you forgive me?"

For once, Sloth's answer was fast.

"I forgive you," said Sloth.

"No one can be a hero all the time."

"Not *all* the time," said Bat,
who liked being a hero.
"But *most* of the time."

"Good morning, Sloth. Sweet dreams."

"Good morning, Bat," said Sloth.

ZZAahhchhhzzz.